THE MIDDLE KINGDOM

Aviv Geva

ISBN: 9781687483515

Cover design by: Esti Nissan
Library of Congress Control Number: 2018675309
Printed in the United States of America

PROLOGUE

First and foremost, let us begin

By stating that the red banana kingdom was ruled by King Brin.

Wild bananas grew in orange, green and yellow,

In brown and even ocean blue, deep and mellow.

But Brin's kingdom was renowned in the jungle far and wide

For the red bananas that grew in the north and along the eastern side.

And so I will commence, but please keep in mind

That the red banana grove was the most important of its kind.

There it was, so close to the eastward entry.

Oh yes! The Holy Grove! Well-guarded by King Brin's loyal primate sentry.

By the monkeys of the jungle he was exceedingly admired.

To populate his kingdom all types and sorts of primates aspired.

Held in great esteem by monkeys a great distance from his realm,

They would occasionally visit the blessed land that held him at the helm.

Forms have to be completed before entry is granted,

For a brief glorious hour, to view the wonder and be enchanted.

A remarkable wonder, a masterpiece, a sign no doubt,

The very spot where the first red banana in the jungle began to sprout!

Much has been said, and will be said, of the singular nature of this dominion.

The stamping ground makes fine peat, the green shoots flourish, branching out,

Perfectly intertwined, the very best for climbing, in everyone's opinion.

Yet distant is the day when throughout the kingdom a black cloud shall spread,

Transforming waterholes filled to the brim into mired bogs, muddy and dead.

Abundant superlatives praise the monkeys' equanimity,

With a salute they acknowledge their persona's sublimity.

Rest assured! Far and wide this fact is known and well construed,

Rare is the day when pique and fury will blacken their mood.

There was no indication of what lay in store,

Of what that week would transpire, changing eternity as never before.

1

On that day, upon the most esteemed tree of all,
Three monkeys sat by rank and order, proud and tall.

Foremost was the sovereign king in royal isolation,
With two eminent monkeys in front, in triangular formation.

One was portly, paunchy and healthfully strong,
Attired in an old ornate vest that was fashionably wrong.

His one eye awake and open wide,
The other, lethargic and drooping aside.

He rifles through his monkey trouser pockets every little while,
Trousers that, by primate fashion rules, have long been out of style.

Anyway, and since you wish to ascertain,
He answers to Pigletti, which is his given name.

Describing the third monkey is not a task that slight.
He is the perfect contrast to the monkey at his right.

Trim of body, endlessly tall and impressively thin,

His primate crest perfectly groomed, and a tie affixed to his double-breasted shirt

with a fashionable pin.

Burakrati is in charge of the travel permits hall,

Receiving letters and postcards that never stop at all,

That come from further away than far, from monkeys of every type and brew.

White monkeys, red monkeys, yellow monkeys, brown, dark brown and blue.

Even light blue and black monkeys too!

Those very same all share one common burning desire, one chore -

For a brief moment to view where the miracle had happened thousands of years before.

Needless to say, that paunchy monkey amused himself and took his chances,

From his high and privileged perch among the branches.

King Brin was much beloved, revered and absolutely good,

But too busy with his many royal tasks to track the goings-on in his kingly neighborhood.

Thus, the Burakrat did as he pleased to his heart's desire,

Boasting of the obstacles he set in the innocent monkeys' path into the empire.

And those who came from afar and even further away,

To ease their arduous entrance desired, as destitute were they.

Yet, an almost royal welcome was extended, without reluctance,

To the primates and monkeys rich with considerable abundance.

Alternately, the rulers of far-away lands had all the right connections,

And a smart monkey knew with whom to nurture excellent relations.

Brin was greatly fond of red bananas, they were his main delight.

In his youth he slugged and brawled in many a great fight.

He recalled how the black monkeys came from the east and western kingdom in droves,

And tried to seize and take over all the great expansive red banana groves.

The black monkeys did not lack for red bananas in any number,

For the jungle was bountiful with bananas of every kind and color.

Bananas outside Brin's kingdom were also abundant and easily found,

So as to the coveting of Brin's own wondrous grove there really was no ground.

But it was those very red bananas that the black monkeys sought.

For it was a black one who, ages past, sowed the first seed, as their legend taught.

That was why into the kingdom's holy places they would stealthily come in,

And were considered an enemy of the kingdom of Brin.

Entering the red banana grove to wreak havoc, just so,

Disturb the red monkeys' enjoyment of their harvest, and then go.

The coal-black monkeys' leaders had intrigues of their own,

Holding secret summit meetings with Brin and his colleagues alone.

Bananas were in profusion and they were so tired of battling,

It seemed so foolish over semantics now to keep on haggling.

First and foremost, a primate of great eminence, Nabucotti is his name,

Who has strong secret ties with king Brin, that very one and the same.

So secretive, that only the guardian angel knew, perhaps by chance,

How the two gazed at the vast groves at a precise hour from that very tree, that very branch.

So very precise and so exact, that far into eternity

This tree would be their sanctuary, their shelter from disparity.

The stirring splendor of secrets was whispered in this treetop cove,

About reconciliation and the division of this highly cherished grove.

About the impish monkeys in Brin's kingdom much will be told,

Of the many colors and varieties residing there, lo and behold!

And they all share in common one vital trait,

They are red banana monkeys, on every tree, in every state.

These are the true facts to which we aspire -

The jungle is vast and full of banana groves, all red as fire.

And precisely for that reason, in many and sundry places,

Live the red banana monkeys, with their infinitely many graces.

Without question, Brin's kingdom is their natural habitat,

They come and they go, and the Burakrat has no say on that.

For, just like him, they are monkeys of the red banana kind.

Their color, nature or cause of visit are irrelevant, he pays no mind.

There is one more tidbit of redundant information -

At times they seem a bit different from the rest of the population.

The monkeys who visit Brin's kingdom from faraway lands, where most of the monkeys are abundantly white,

Resemble them closely, but they too are red banana monkeys, just to set things right.

So it matters not that the red banana monkeys who come to Brin's kingdom from the great deep jungle, the black monkeys' habitat,

Are mostly brown in color, and even dark brown at that.

And some surreptitiously will claim, for spite,

That they are in fact and without a doubt as black as the blackest night.

None of this will affect a change, herein lies the dictum:

The red banana monkeys will be forever welcome

To visit the magical grove and reside within Brin's kingdom.

But let it be said that the brown monkeys, and the very dark brown too,

Dislike the black monkeys, in that there's nothing new.

It is probably due to the fact

That they similarly behave and react,

Both black and brown, the dark brown most markedly,

To the red bananas that they all love so ardently.

Their love and craving are of such nature and passion

That without these adored bananas, their life would seem ashen!

King Brin was a white monkey, he was white in hue.

Yet he loved red bananas and prized them too.

But from the summit of his wisdom and years, his respect grew and grew

For bananas that were brown, yellow, green or orange, and even blue.

Most white monkeys loved the blue bananas that grew in rich ground

At the western tip of the kingdom, where the great waterhole was found.

It was mostly the white monkeys who sat on the royal throne,

Though brown and even dark brown monkeys could always claim it as their own.

But the latter were too preoccupied with the struggle and protection

Of the magical red banana grove, what an absolute perfection!

And if, for a moment, you thought red bananas are not to the white monkey's liking,

Then, quite the opposite is true, your mistake is most striking!

The finest of the white monkeys over the red fruit stood sentry,

But so that others wouldn't know, they did so covertly.

More than its love of the red fruit, the public wanted most, in all candor,

To follow the directives from Pigletti, their beloved commander.

Don't get me wrong, make no mistake at all,

This is not about that four-legged domestic animal.

His nose is flat, his skin a pinkish tone.

He imposes awe and terror, together and alone.

The commander-in-chief of the kingdom, understand,

Is the great general, and the king's right hand.

He must maintain order and harmonious accord,

But he first must have structure, chaos he cannot afford.

A single monkey, though with a plethora of white monkeys all around,

Cannot control a kingdom in which all kinds and types of monkeys abound.

Thus, two group leaders from Brin's kingdom were always at his side.

One was Rusty Jed, who was chief of the red monkeys' tribe.

The very same tribe that fully believed that due to their red color,

It is they alone who are most closely linked to the red bananas, and no other.

Furthermore, and most essentially, they are bound

To the eternal red banana grove by the reddest blood ever to be found!

It is no fabrication, no tale nor fable -

They shall never relinquish a single red banana. They aren't able.

The second aide, Obscurati was his name, had excellent relations

With the blue and light-blue monkey tribes, who followed his dictations.

Befriending him as well was the Burakrat, and he too

Was a blue-blooded monkey, though his color was pale whitish-blue.

Now let us not ignore this rhyme,

A tale is to be told, important and sublime!

🐵

A new day in the forest awakens.
The bear whispers and the butterfly beckons.

As the pact far and wide entreats,
Listen close and be silent, the poet speaks.

Its power shall be swept away by the winds,
Its language crushed, as with the dust it rescinds.

A dark cloud the blue heavens will quell,
On the day the skies descend from hell.

The crescent shall rise and the sun shall fade,
From a distance observed, in the heavens inlaid.

A torrential rain for days on end
Through every crack and crevice its way will wend.

The skies shall darken like a millennium ago
And massive waves from cliffs shall flow.

How shall we move on if this does not cease,
A lad named Joseph will the question release.

He tightened his belt round the coat he wore,
From gravel and stone his heart shall soar.

In the vast space behind, a convoy slithers,
Like endless columns of ants it dithers.

And with it the very same question is posed,
Of "how" and of "why" and what it supposed.

Its source shall be duly noted aloud,
In the torrential rain, the flood and cloud.

From afar it appears like the eyes of a hawk,
Showered in flames, and as yellow as yolk.

He raises his head to understand,
A red burning bush on a mound of sand.

The innocent lad will awaken and say,
Teach us some more, united we stay.

The pact was consecrated, its roots grew deep,

Jacob's eternity, the kingdom will keep.

2

It all began with a stomach ache much derided,
But, oh, the wonder and greatness it provided!

"Most likely a red banana that I ate with the break of day",
Brin moaned lightly as the daily state meeting got under way.

On the agenda, general banana issues, as on every day,
The shortage of finer tree branches from which to sway,
And foreign relations with the white monkeys far away.

Sometimes discussion centered on the yellow monkeys, not so distant,
With whom the red banana monkeys' discords were persistent.

"Are you sure it was a banana of the red variety?"
Asked incredulously his aide, Burakrati.

These red bananas were the kingdom's crowning glory.
How could they possibly, one bright morning,
Cause Brin a belly ache without any warning?!

"Your words are well spoken", Brin replied. "As I was climbing up the great assembly tree on my way here,

It may certainly have been a banana of the orange variety that I
ate, I fear."

Then returned at once to the agenda at hand,

As they assembled at the treetop, so high and grand.

Pigletti was displeased with what he'd just heard.

His leader's words seemed to him quite absurd.

How could his beloved leader, the wisest of all,

Utter such words that shock and appall?

And so he reflected between himself and he,

Never revealing what his thoughts may be.

A red banana can cause stomach aches and pain?

Never in our kingdom! That is certainly insane!

Our great King Brin knows as well as the next

That red bananas are forever nutritious and the very best.

And all will agree our king's brilliance is unswerving.

No word of his is wasted, or ever undeserving.

Could it possibly be that deep down in his heart,

The king is harboring thoughts that chafe and smart?

Could our wonderful, beloved monarch question

Or besmirch the red bananas as a source of indigestion?

Perhaps if he continues this point to ponder...

No, no, this thought must change and move on yonder.

Could our illustrious leader possibly cast doubt in his heart
Upon the red banana monkeys' nature, even in part???

"Ahem, ahem, my divine king",
The Piglet cleared his throat as he turned to Brin.
"Another report has come in, of a gang of Blacks who in our northern kingdom invaded a grove.
To bring about ruin and destruction they strove.
They were four in number, and badly assailed
A red monkey female who was injured and flailed!
For our traditions and culture they have no respect,
And to share our red bananas with them they expect.
Their impertinence on this matter I fully reject!"

"Absolutely so and I fully agree", Brin replied reflectively.
"We must take the harshest measures", he went on agreeably.

"Yes, my king. Obscurati's flying monkeys ended the altercation
And seized the black banana trees in a nearby location.
Thus every black monkey will fully understand,
We shall respond and counter-fight, if they invade our land!"

He then raised his hand upward in dramatic retort,
But Brin's serious expression cut his gesture short.

In his great wisdom Brin preferred, if possible, to avoid invasion

Of other monkey lands, and with pirate tribes he applied the same evasion.

He learned this well from his experience so vast,
As commander of the Order of the Crown, in the past.

In that cursed time the black monkeys tried repeatedly
To seize and hold the kingdom's red banana groves at the periphery.

For the Reds it was quite burdensome, yet indispensable,
As all they wanted was to protect their grove so very magical.

For at every dawn, or in the dead of night,
The Blacks from the periphery vandalized with all their might.

Thus, for every young monkey that climbed the wrong tree
And chewed on a banana with appetite and glee,
The royal troops hastened to attack his family and friends,
And quickly seized those red banana groves to make amends.

Otherwise these red bananas would be forever lost,
A situation that must be prevented at all cost!

In consequence, delegates from distant regions, and not-so-distant ones especially,
Rushed to the kingdom to express their vexation ad hoc most mindfully.

A wave of grievances against the red banana kingdom swelled,

Demonstrations and marches soon had to be quelled.

The not-so-distant monkeys could send their herds of great elephants to roam
For some days down the great mountain slopes, before returning home,
Devastating, not deliberately for sure, the kingdom's land and loam.

"Return the black banana trees at once!" Brin instructed and orders sent.
"We must apply restraint and judgment", he said, much to the Piglet's discontent.

"We certainly are not a pirate tribe, to that we must endeavor!
Violence will erode the foundations of our kingdom forever!
That is not who we are, that is not our route.
Through peaceful means we will resolve our dispute."

He forcefully pounded the branch of the tree,
Nearly causing an unfortunate fall of all three.

Perhaps it's the banana that Brin ate at dawn, reflected Pigletti,
Which is the culprit after all. He then stole a glance at Burakrati,
Who seemed somewhat detached from the stately meeting,
Yet displeased with the instructions that Brin was emitting.

Since when do the Blacks deserve such considerate fair play?
Pigletti kept wondering, hiding signs of dismay.

They are nothing but barbarians, it's a well-established fact,
Out to spread destruction and venom, leaving nothing intact.

And if it were our Holy Grove that was under invasion,
Would our king still preach restraint and consideration?

Oh no, it is completely idiotic,
I won't even harbor a thought so chaotic!

"Well done, well done, Your Majesty.
I shall pass it on straight away to Obscurati."

But first, the Piglet secretly decided, I will give the command
To destroy all those trees, so these villains will know where they stand.

He straightened his tie, nodding his head most chivalrously,
Then left in haste, bounding through the tree branches dexterously.

The words were pronounced,
And war was announced.

The abomination shall become devastation
And treason shall be born of the invasion.

In his twilight days, he was none the sager,

Understanding no better the terrible failure,

How it had all turned to dust,
How misplaced was his trust.

Like a black shadow cast by a cloak,
Darkness shall cover the earth in a stroke.

From abysmal depths resurrection shall rise,
The crescent moon will shed light from the skies.

At present, King Brin is the sentinel on guard,
His mind from left and from right is jarred

By an abundance of consultants of every color,
Whose tongues grow sharp as their minds grow duller.

But the king is attuned to his thoughts down deep,
Sharing naught with others, with himself to keep.

3

At high noon of that very hot day

Three monkeys sat in a primate circle, and very red were they.

The first, the Jedic, Rusty Jed,

The second. whose brow with deep furrows was tread,

The third with a mane as curly as an endive leaf,

All three now sat together in a circular motif.

All three monkeys were deeply immersed

In daily primate issues and heartily conversed.

They drank wild grape nectar and many red bananas did they ingest,

Then reclined on a nearby bush, awaiting their nearing hour of rest.

"This is an especially red day", said the curly-head.

"Yes, yes", the furrowed brow agreed, "indeed, very red."

"Long live the red and its eternally beloved sacred grove!"

Curly-head roared and joyfully jumped and began to rove.

"Silence, you fools!" the Jed quickly hushed them. "Do you think your intoxicated shouts are what is advisable

To keep our magical grove forever viable?

Absolutely not and the answer is no!"

He yelled, while they looked dazed, as if after a blow.

"There are many monkeys in our kingdom, most of them white,

Who've long deserted what we hold most dear in our sight.

And what may that be, you reddish primates?" He asked to ascertain.

"The grove! The grove!" Curly Head cheered as the Brow hit him with pain.

"Silence, you blubbering fool! Don't yelp!

How do you think your shouting will help?

Most red banana monkeys are busy with their daily chores and have long forgotten the taste of that sacred banana, that very one!

Residing along the banks of the great waterhole with worries none,

Eating nothing but blue bananas in the sun!

And rumor has it that our beloved king, most adored …"

"Adored! Adored!" Curly exclaimed and again was slapped by the Brow in reward.

"Even our king, most wise and beloved throughout the land,

Whose wisdom spans forests, mountains and bogs of sand,

Whose greatness spreads far and wide the kingdom through,

Chews with great pleasure on bananas that are blue.

Such mastication is becoming more frequent with time,

Cursed be the day he forgets the red banana's taste sublime!"

"Curse the day! Curse the day! Curse the day?" Curly glanced at Rusty Jed,

While the Brow looked their way, fell silent and gazed ahead.

"We must commiserate, my primate colleagues",

He whispered mysteriously, hinting at shady intrigues.

"A tactic so bold and so clever,

That the red banana monkeys will cognize they are the Reds, it's their life's essence forever!

Now hurry and assemble many and all of the Reds to here!

Our task is great and to our obligation we'll adhere!

But take care to explain, in a manner somewhat furtive,

The assembly is routine, let there be no hint of a hidden motive.

The grove and its sanctity are the focus, the main thrust,

The assembly's objective. That's crystal clear, I trust?"

"Clear as crystal! Crystal clear!" Curly rushed to affirm and salute,

As the Brow raised himself heavily without dispute.

How dare our colleague allow such words in his repertoire?

Disparaging our beloved leader so! Perhaps he's gone too far?

But surely not, it all must have a perfectly logical explanation.

I too am a red monkey and, as to Rusty Jed, I must refrain from deprecation.

For, certainly and clearly, our grove is consecrated!

I will conduct myself so, instruct others and to the mission stay dedicated.

The Jed's desire I will now fulfill,
Though my eyes are only half-open still.

Yes, yes, I will conduct myself accordingly,
And follow the master wisely and sportingly.

"Long live Brin and his red kingdom forever!"
He boomed, as the Curly repeated, just to sound clever.

"Long live Brin! Long live the kingdom forever!
Long live the grove, it shall never end, ever!"

King Brin was advanced in years, and well he knew
That his days were numbered and very few.

It was his task the Middle Kingdom to defend,
His glorified reform, at the angel's command.

He boldly gazed out at the horizon to discern
The enemy drawing near, with growing concern.

Throughout the city there was partying and jubilation,
With revelers in a lustful mood, free of any obligation.

The Gilead trees with their cone-shaped leaves
Have long been felled, there are no retrieves.

To redeem them his powers no longer suffice,
But perhaps to abate from all hellish device.

With the passage of time a deed shall be done,
The promise kept, though others the deed may shun.

Another option, without a doubt,
Is to break that promise and crush it out.

But such an act cannot be implemented,
And the king himself to leave tormented.

To silence the celebrators in the village square,
Imprison the traitor and observe his despair.

Another day ends, fifty years transpire,
The scroll shall be written, its saga as fervent as fire.

4

"Yes, yes, long live the Grove", muttered one very reddish ape in muted sound,

While to the legendary golden grove his steps were bound.

"Such ignoramuses as these for millennia haven't been seen on this very ground."

"The gate is to be opened at once and with a salute!"

A screeching yell so loud was heard, to turn one deaf and mute,

As the reddish Jed was loudly pacing

Towards the gate, made of great pinewood interlacing.

"Open up! Quickly now!" he shouted as he was about to walk through.

"Bring the finest bananas, crimson red, deep maroon, and finely wrapped too!"

"The very best, wrapped and ready, one-two-three!"

The guard on duty repeated loudly and emphatically.

"This is a special day of celebration, its importance uncontested,

On this day the most delicious, tastiest bananas must be ingested!"

He pointed proudly to that same banana bunch so grand,
Arranged in an impressive wrapping, snuggled nicely in his hand.

"Now be on your guard, stay alert and keep your eyes peeled!
Prevent all harm to this holy site especially, protect it and shield!"

"It shall be done, revered commander!"
The primate sentries responded in full candor.

"Stay safe and vigilant remain",
He replied and was quick to disappear again.

The bedecked banana bunch was quite heavy in weight,
After a monkeyly-while he reached the black moon-faced monkeys' prayer site, with a heavy gait.

The minister knocked on doors and jumped about,
Till one black monkey through a tiny tree-trunk window peeked out.

Though he seemed so young, his feelings ran strong,
And quickly began shouting that something was wrong:

"Red! Red! Here he comes for us to harm!"
The tree was abuzz with frenzied alarm.

Black ruffians in response rushed towards the entrance way,
Keeping any logic or common sense at bay.

"Stop at once, I so command!"

A moderate voice ordered the ruffians to disband.

"I alone towards the entry shall advance,

To clarify and learn the circumstance.

Return to your prayers promptly as required!

I will later fully share with you all that has transpired."

For heaven's sake! This is no time for riots! His heart was pained.

What more will this day bring, how will it be explained?

"Red! Red!" The young one kept shouting and was quickly removed from the window's ledge.

"Carry on with your prayers!", the elder instructed and slowly advanced to the threshold's edge.

"Good Sir, Nabuccotti, most respected and revered!",

The Jedic's words were spoken when at the door he appeared.

"Welcome, my red friend, and may you be blessed.

We are most honored to receive such a venerated guest!

No messenger or high-ranking officer did you send",

He blessed the mandate figure and continued to commend.

"It would be most unfitting, would it not, a messenger to send,

And this auspicious occasion I myself would not attend?"

He replied, before the dark monkey continued to chat.

"This gift is from the most honored and wise, and from his groves at that!"

"From King Brin, the one and the same?", the moon-faced monkey in wonder exclaimed.

"We are most honored, may every blessing upon him be proclaimed."

"But quickly, share this gift with the little ones and now!

Our friendship from the bottom up will flower, I avow!

For brothers are we, make no mistake of that, oh no!

On this holiday, eat and be joyous, let the festivities flow!"

"No words to express our thanks can suffice!"

The dark moon-faced monkey with humility said twice.

"You will explain to the beloved Brin, I trust,

A new forest will be illumined, as discussed!"

"Indeed it shall be relayed!" Rusty Jed was quick to say,

"And to the little ones, to the little ones hand out!" he shouted as he rushed away.

But as the door was shut, his voice was barely heard,

For the dark leader's mind with peculiar thoughts now whirred.

This is somewhat dubious, he reflected on the matter.

When they last conversed, it was nothing more than discrete patter.

The Jedic said, share with the young, between us there is no divide,

And it is Brin who sends his blessings, with his best wishes us has dignified!

Can it be that he is so esteemed, that in no time whatsoever,
The Reds' disfavor of the Blacks he has succeeded thus to lever?

This Rusty Jed holds a very high position,
And the crimson red bananas are holy for the Reds by definition!

Brin is probably too preoccupied to travel such a distance,
And instead his esteemed envoy sent. "Bring in the infants!"
The leader elatedly cried out. "Eat the red bananas and with them delight!
Mete them out to each and every one, to anyone in sight!"

In his eye a tear arose, born of disbelief,
"As the minister said, a holiday it is!" he shouted with relief.

"A new forest will illumine, a forest new and bright",
Murmured the reddish Jed as he hopped along in the approaching night.
What was it the two discussed with such seriousness and gravity?
My thoughts are so disturbing, they are challenging my sanity.

But as he hopped along, his agitation grew.
Why a new forest? What good will it do?

The current forest with its beauty, does it not suffice?
Need we with the moon-faced Blacks a better forest to devise?

And the eagerness with which he took those bananas, so swift!

As if he were expecting with the break of dawn the arrival of a gift.

So nice of him not to grumble that time had nearly gone adrift!

But with the zephyr's growing gusts of wind,

He stopped deliberating, his calculations dimmed.

His elongated arms now far outstretched,

The strongest boughs to grasp he quickly fetched.

So as not to fall again as happened just a year before,

And his missus had to do the feeding and cleaning and every other chore.

And throughout that year it was her duty as well

To pick and gather those deeply red bananas that were so swell.

And once a month to the magical grove she would make haste,

Then recount to the Jedic all that transpired, with great detail laced.

But nothing was the same when the weary Red was not around,

No curly-head or simpleton could do the job for which he was renowned.

But soon this reminiscence with himself he stopped recounting,

As he rushed to Pigletti to give a full accounting.

Quickly and agilely he swung from one branch to the next.

The Piglet, as always, will resolve things for the best.

The red is holy, and most sanctified is the site.

He need only tell the Piglet and all will be set right.

🛕

Hundreds and thousands of years shall pass,
And deep-growing roots in the earth shall amass.

A new era shall then emerge,
The past will not be forsaken, time the past won't purge.

The demon's shadow from the ancient past
Will appear on this day, his image recast.

Be not tempted to trust him, make no mistake,
Recall his past actions, stay strong and awake,

For he cannot abandon the people once more.
Foster strength and rebuild the nation as before.

And if these words be forgotten ever,
My covenant with thee shall be erased forever.

I am the One, but shall never speak.
Stand by me, I shall never grow weak.

The seed shall spread like countless grains of sand,
I am the One and no other, tall and strong I stand.

5

One black monkey keeps pacing to and fro,
As thoughts fill his mind and will not let go.

One singular focus he has now lost himself in,
The black groves at the northern edge of the kingdom of Brin.

Among the convoluted branches of the cedar tree on high,
He sits well concealed from the watchful sentries' eye.

Holding small round binoculars and never growing tired,
He spends days and nights observing all that has transpired.

Here, just the other day, the Reds did not refrain
From coming down and devastating their cultivated grain.

Just because the little ones wanted to have some fun,
And swung on the red banana trees, till some damage there was done!

There was no hope, it was long ago lost,
And he was determined now to change things at all cost.

Full of tricks and ruses, this northern black had a talent for guile,
The Reds will be taught a painful lesson, it will be worthwhile!

Nabucotti only dreams of peace and what it may bring,
And cannot see a thing beyond the contemptible Brin the king!

Beneath the tree, like sentinels in a military operation,
Black monkeys stand row after row in perfect formation.

They share one single goal for which they mobilize,
With animosity and hatred burning in their eyes.

"Listen closely, harken to what I say.
With giant steps we are drawing closer to Judgment Day!

The bruised little ones your own eyes have seen.
The Reds rejoiced in your defeat, your spirits to demean!

The blackened trees were reclaimed by their advances,
And not a single banana did they leave on the branches.

Humiliating the young ones, creating chaos and disorder,
Telling us, 'Go to your black brothers at the jungle's border!'

But oh no, we shall not leave.
Red bananas by the thousands our hands will crush and cleave!

The time of judgment is growing near,
We're no longer sitting on the fence, that's clear!

On the trees, few or many, we will never compromise,
And our red-black essence we shall cherish like a prize.

From the northern kingdom we will commence
And reclaim our honor at the great waterhole, whatever the expense!

Destruction and ruin will be left in our trail
On our way to the Grove, holy to us as well!

And the moon-faced Blacks will know nothing of this,
They are like Joseph's dim-witted brothers who went amiss.

They've filled their dark heads with a silly dream,
That they'll get their fair share from the venerated King Brin!

What possible reason would he have to divide and share?
His lands are peaceful, he is free of care.

Until they get their taste of the dreadful and bitter,
To share with us ever so slightly they will never consider.

With our great black power we will force them to flee!
Into the great waterhole, and then – into the sea!

With speed to the great waterhole now we must head,

Devastation of the blue bananas to spread!

Such damage will certainly leave its mark,
And among the red monkeys confusion will spark.

And as they engage in fighting each other,
We will then strike them down without much bother!

Off with their heads, let their blood flow a red river,
As the magical grove to our very own hands we deliver!"

Hoorahs were shouted from far and near,
Worshipping Norde, the Agagic lord they held so dear.

Reddish Blacks they are, after all, and certain are they
That their historic claims to the red bananas all others outweigh.

It was perfectly clear to them now, they will not stray,
They will obey him to the letter on the great Judgment Day.

No longer will the Reds' harsh insults be tolerated,
Nor will they remain on the northern border, frustrated.

For this is the time and this is the hour
To change the jungle forever, through struggle and power.

Rows upon rows of cavaliers sit tall and tight,

Like an endless trail as black as night.

Their brows are evil, their sweat is cold,
Their armor is steel, their daggers bold.

Without any promise they came to the land,
To destroy and demolish was the task at hand.

For the officers in the lead the situation was clear,
The king thinks that from them he's got nothing to fear.

But their message will be sounded far and wide,
Traversing the seas, with no place to hide.

With mounting power the lands they will seize,
Conquer the Middle Kingdom, bring the Reds to their knees.

He shall not weaken nor falter, nor waver from his path,
Till the Middle Kingdom is obliterated forever through his wrath.

That will end the rumor with no further delay,
That to those the land was promised. We will do and obey.

6

At precisely the advocated hour, in the depths of the tree-filled grove,
Reddish Reds gathered, protesting against nothing special, drove by drove.

Their red blood was seething, but one grey cloud floating in the sky
Would suffice to cool them off with a light shower from on high.

"Get into line! Get into line to honor our sovereign king!"
The one with the furrowed brow barked out, overseeing everything.

"And be silent!" ordered his colleague immediately after,
His frizzly hair wild, as he shouted to please the master.

His head was so dense with curls, it looked from afar
Like a grubby ball, big and bizarre.

Just then the Jed on his speech was about to embark,
As he savored the flavor of a banana, red crimson dark.

Excellent, he thought to himself, most pleased.

They are all here before me, with great anger seized.

There is nothing left for me to do
But scowl and their hearts with fear imbue.

Curly and the Brow nothing will comprehend,
Their stupidity is great, but they'll serve my purpose till the end.

I will shock them now to such an extent,
Upon trauma I am bent, even the wisest won't know what I meant.

In a moment I'll stand before them and address them with coherence.
Just another bite of the banana, and I begin my dramatic appearance.

"Silence now, absolute silence! Our grand minister is here!"
The Brow, with his deep furrows, called out in a tone severe.

The beads of sweat trickling at fast pace
Seemed more like gushing brooks coursing down his face.

Just then, with light but deliberate paces,
The Reds' venerated minister entered, gazing at the sea of faces.

In the bald space among the grand oak trees a great silence fell,
As each one waited to hear what their leader had to tell.

To the demand for silence they paid such heed,

That one red monkey gulped the rest of his banana down with speed.

And he was careful that no hiccup would then follow,

That no sound would break the silence just because he had to swallow.

Rusty Jed began his speech with the words, "Beloved Reds!"

"I am the bearer of sad news!", at which some began to whisper, others shook their heads.

Perhaps our head-of-state has fallen ill,

Or our beloved king has taken sick, worse still!

"Silence!" Curly roared and shouted,

"Pay attention to our leader whose words are undoubted!"

"My dear children, do not bow your heads",

The grand leader continued addressing the Reds,

"My eyes! How could my eyes witness such a dreadful scene?!

The choice is no longer ours, after something so obscene!

As red as scarlet and crimson were they!

With my own eyes I saw the scarlet and crimson that day!

And the banana peels, those peels like trash were strewn!

The little ones crushed them, that no one can impugn!

The moon-faced ones have determined our fate!

Sentence has been passed. We must no longer wait!

With my very own eyes I saw them eat more and more!

And the peels like trash were strewn on the floor!"

A shudder shook the primate bodies of the crimson Reds.
A most hideous crime, the very same thought entered their heads.

The moon-faced Blacks have declared war, forced us into combat.
Nothing will ever satisfy them in their very own habitat!

To destroy and humiliate us, to them nothing else matters.
Letting their young ones break and crush banana peels into tatters.

Just one single primate scratched his head, his thoughts began to falter,
And from his furrowed brow kept streaming down rivulets of water.

How is it that our lofty Jed is telling this just now?
When with Curly we all three met, none of it did he avow!

Only now, before an eager crowd that is mostly ignorant,
Does he allow himself to inform us of events so belligerent.

Just look at that curly-headed one, jumping around like an insane,
Not a single intelligent thought is to be found in his small brain.

Yet how can I raise such doubts and suspicion?
Or disparage our leader's words and elevated position??

At once, I must erase such thoughts from my mind,

I am of junior rank, can't think anything of the kind!

Fate has dealt me a good hand, I should really feel elated,

Unlike the trembling crowd, my position is quite elevated.

I will go on pondering, but keep my thoughts concealed,

Answering "yea" to our commander, keeping my lips well sealed.

"And the dark browns, where were they when the bananas were stolen on their watch?"

The reddish Jed continued his fire-and-brimstone speech, raising it up a notch.

"Or perhaps they lost their senses and forgot about our treasure trove,

Thinking it was a holiday, distributing free presents from our Holy Grove!"

"Holy! Holy!" shouted the Reds along with their mentor,

While the impassioned Curly Head kept jumping in the center.

"But let us not rush into action!"

The reddish Jed announced with passion.

"Now return to your trees, stay calm and collected,

Instructions will follow, we will do as directed!"

"Ready we are, Sir!" the Curly shouted, with the crowd in his wake.

Then some simple-minded monkeys started brawls, for fighting's sake.

"There shall be no fighting amongst us ever!"
The Red shouted, loving his success and feeling clever.

"Wait patiently for the command, resume your occupation,
And as to the matter at hand, pay no heed for the duration.

"Now scatter quickly to your habitats among the trees.
Be blessed on your way, and guard your secret please!"

"Blessed be you on your way, dear Reds,
And before our exalted leader let us now bow our heads!"

Bellowed the curly-headed primate with the frizz,
As the Brow dispersed the masses like a whizz.

Rusty Jed stepped back, happy and content,
Munching on a very black banana with jubilant intent.

The mountain cannot be cut through, not ever,
Young and old will climb to the top with endeavor.

On the slopes of Gilead they engage in battle without fear,
Inundated by the wave till the one and only will appear.

Warriors will strike and the enemy shall overtake,
Crushed under horses' hoofs, felled by the venom of a snake.

That very day the voice of God is heard,
Reconfirming His message with every word.

On that day I shall descend for the very last time,
And the flood as prophesied will dominate the clime.

Listen closely to what your soul imparts,
Silence your tongues and soften your hearts.

Nothing exists but the words I have spoken,
You are pure, you are all my children.

On that day every safeguard must be in place,
I shall hold you close to me in an eternal embrace.

The foreign one to you I shall send,
To be your support, your brother and friend.

And on that day, as these words he decrees,
He gazes from on high, it is no dream that he sees.

With crowned heads in the desert they advance,
And the invisible seems to appear in the sands.

I shall open your eyes and lift you on high,
No statues or mountains shall you deify.

The gold is to be smashed, crushed and broken,
Like every obstacle, like a useless token.

He who blesses you is leading you astray,
From his lofty position he will corrupt and betray.

Listen to my words, to this my brief appeal,
For truth and justice nothing can conceal.

For eternal generations your way shall go on,
Forever your seed will see a new dawn.
Take the Book, read in it and tell,
And gently, without fear, repeat it well.

By right of a covenant that I have made with thee,
Through Abraham and Isaac, for all eternity.

7

That night, the moon-faced Black found no peaceful sleep,
His thoughts exhausted him, his worries ran deep.

For just the other day he sat with the king sharing a branch,
And no word was said of a gift of any kind or chance.

Though the reddish Jed holds a very high position,
He isn't fond at all of taking any grave decision.

As to the gift, there certainly was reason to feel deep shame.
For not sending a gift to the king in return he had but himself to blame.

But these were not the heavy thoughts that pounded in his brain,
It was his subjects' restlessness that surfaced once again.

Rumor has it that the Agagic Norte is fomenting trouble and enmity,
Slandering Brin and rendering him his enemy.

His black visage in appeasement has no stake,
His every action seeks out quarrels for destruction's sake.

There is no choice but to rise at dawn and sort it all out.
Brin is no less than a brother, a friend, without a doubt.

And those young pupils must be taught another lesson,
They must listen and adopt a totally new direction.

They must know that Brin the king is a loving man of peace,
By no means is he the enemy, that thought must quickly cease!

At dawn the moon-faced monkey rose and made his bed,
His heart filled with prayer for the day ahead.

A sermon like none other he must deliver without delay,
And talk to the young like grown-ups, not like kids at play.

For we are happy with our lot and certainly need no more,
The way to peace is far better than the path of war!

Brin understands this well, as only the finest of primates could,
And often whispered so in his ear on that very branch in the wood.

We must act slowly, no conspiracy's involved.
The matter is complex and wisely needs to be resolved.

The kingdom of Brin consists of many different clans,
Reds, blues, yellows, whites and browns living on the lands.

And each clan holds its own point of view

On the holiness of the grove, and on its neighbors too.

But that promise has taken root deep in his heart,
The day of a bright new forest is near, time for a new start!

Peace will not be gained by actions done in haste,
A myriad of initial steps must first be wisely paced.

The mission is intricate and complicated,
The young ones must be quickly congregated.

It is the young ones who their elders will inform,
As the elders' minds are weakened and unwilling to reform.

To wait and see what comes – that cannot be said,
But our hope rests with the young ones for what lies ahead!

And Norte must hear nothing of this, for their minds he will surely mire,
And I his foe will be if he knows how much I trust Brin and him admire.

"Gather round, my little followers", says the senior Black as he stands
And picks up a mischievous little monkey in his hands.
"Today is such a lovely day,
And time to listen closely to what I have to say."

All the little monkeys at the granary sat near,
Whispering, leaping about and curious to hear.

What does their most eminent leader want to tell?
This is indeed a lucky day, and it is going well!

"Look around you, children, at this place you call home.
We live in peace, have all we need and never have to roam.
There is nothing more for us to crave,
But our home to protect, standing as one and brave!
We have many friends, of different color and hue,
And they have objects and places and a structure too."
"The grove, the grove!", the little one spoke out.
"No, it is not blessed, it is the devil's work about!"

How could our leader hold forth against us like this?
The young ones were shocked, something was amiss.

From their day of birth, they had to learn and comprehend,
To the grove aspire, forever and ever, without end!

'The devil's work', the leader is telling the youth,
Could their very own parents have told an untruth???

"Beloved children, listen to me well,
He spreads rumors of war, no good will it foretell.
We beat and were beaten by our friends, the Reds,
Over the red banana groves we all lost our heads!

Now each of you go home, quietly and silent,

Lock this secret in your hearts, on this remain compliant!
Today you are young, but as your age will increase,
You are those who will offer your hands in peace!"

The young ones then scattered to laugh and play,
To climb the tall trees and from the branches sway.

With nightfall the young one who had earlier shouted
Now sat with his folks and the whole story spouted.

"The grove is nothing but a villainous act.
Our senior leader said precisely that.

And thinking of the Reds as our enemy must cease.
They want to live with us in brotherly peace."

His father grumbled, then screamed so loud,
That he shook the tree and their branch slightly bowed.

This very night he will gather the blackest Blacks, determined and bold,
And to the Agagic turn, the decree to uphold.

Their faces cloaked, they stand prepared,
As sharp as falcons, their orders declared.

On that very day, from the gaping abyss

Your demons and angels will not be remiss.

Facing them like a wall, unguarded,
With truncated swords, their commands discarded.

Billows of black vapor from above shall ascend,
From a gaping maw the light shall transcend.

A giant wave shall swell and rise,
Crushing their coaches, their cloaks disguise.

Upon this kingdom no hand shall rise.
Naught shall this promise ever compromise.

Fight to the full ruin of the contender,
Through the gates of the kingdom no serpent shall enter.

This covenant for all eternity shall endure,
Through sweat and blood, and joy secure.

No man shall determine its delineation,
Death awaits he who crosses the demarcation.

The trees are lofty, the skies they sweep,
Exquisite and holy, their roots run deep.

The Reds the land must preserve night and day,
By the holy Word, none shall possess it but they.

8

At this very moment at the crack of dawn,
Before the first light of day did spawn,

A very reddish Jed hops between the trees,
Making his way through the thickets with ease.

He is nearing that tree so very bluish green,
Almost time for the daily conclave to convene.

There is not a single moment to waste,
To his master he must go with haste,
A report to give of the new forest, rephrased.

The Piglet awoke that morning, his good mood erased.
A good night's sleep by vexing thoughts was replaced.

Throughout the night a cold sweat damped his brow.
A frantic shaking took hold of him now.

Clutching the thin treetop branches and not letting go,
He gazes upon the kingdom below.

His eminent position no longer seems desirable.

The complaints and doubts he has to bear have now become intolerable.

Worrisome issues must be handled with care,

Furtively, with cunning, keeping Brin unaware.

Strong gusts of wind through the tree branches hissed

As the darkness of night receded in the mist.

Knew he well what such winds portend,

No good could come from the way they wend.

His thoughts weighed heavy upon him that day,

But the 'why' and the 'wherefore,' he couldn't say.

As his worrisome thoughts kept racing to and fro,

He heard a strange crackling noise from the bushes below.

Peering downward, he was able to detect

Rusty Jed, awake and about, earlier than you'd expect.

"This is the thing", he began without delay,

Spilling out words of what he had to say.

Thus he spoke as the Piglet kept descending

From the glorious treetop, not yet comprehending.

"Slow down, my red-banana-loving friend,

A dark coffee-brown banana now is what I recommend.

It will perk us up, I myself have just awoke,

And you seem to be a most preoccupied bloke!"

The Piglet said with misplaced cheerfulness,

Careful to conceal an elusive anxiousness.

"My dear Pigletti, most esteemed friend,

With most disturbing news we must now contend."

"Disturbing?" he managed to ask while chewing in a manner obscene

On two brown bananas that emitted the scent of caffeine.

"Most disturbing, indeed, as high as the sky",

The Jedic reported breathlessly, ending with a sigh.

He'd made his way that morning as fast as he could,

Not resting for a second in the mist-covered wood.

"You will have to wait", the Piglet said in a decisive tone.

"Your presence at our daily meet will be this one time alone.

Relay your message directly to the king. And if not…"

He lowered his eyes, then looked at Jed, "It cannot be ignored, the news that you've got?"

"Let us head out this minute without delay!

Prepare the kangaroo!" he ordered the royal guard straight away.

The monkey patrol stood alert and prepared
At the foot of that great tree, which to no other compared.

And there is no better time than right now to point out
How this marsupial helped all the 'who's who' to move quickly about.

Its outstanding feature, of course, was its pouch,
In which four or five monkeys could comfortably crouch.

Its splendid hopping created movement at such speed,
That to grasp at high or low branches it clearly had no need.

Of course, in return for the marsupials' services so obligingly compliant,
The monkeys picked the finest treetop leaves upon which they are reliant.
And thanks to this harmony, although bizarre somewhat,
The kangaroos can lie about and fully satiate their stomach and gut.

"Let us not rush, Sir!" pleaded reddish Jed.
"My message was for your ears only, do not be misled!"
"For my ears only?!" The Piglet looked askance.
"How dare you say such foolishness, and not by chance?
I set about to bring you in person to the king.
And yet you dare utter such a distrustful thing?!"

Greatly sad was Pigletti and filled with chagrin.

There would never be secrets between him and Brin.

"No, Sir, you must fully put your trust in me.
The matter at hand is crucial to the greatest degree.
Blasphemy could never ever cross my mind,
But, truly, you should hear me first, be so inclined.
Listen well, reconsider, your thoughts secured,
Approach the king alone, I am your ally, rest assured!"

Two sentinels that moment came before the Piglet to report:
"The royal kangaroo is set and ready to transport!"

They said nothing of his kicking them with his hoofs repeatedly,
Annoyed that they'd awakened and recruited him so heatedly.

"Today, however, his services will not be required.
To bound among the branches on my own I am not too tired."

"Well said, Sir, take it slowly",
The Jedic felt good, his breath restored almost wholly.
"So let me get to the heart of the matter,
And the events that took place, without useless chatter.
As per your instructions of the day before,
I set out to the enchanted grove, to inspect and explore.
While swinging through the holy branches, with red bananas in my hand,
I came across that pitch-black moon-face at the eastern edge of our wonderful land.

"Those moon-faced primates hang out there quite a lot",

The Piglet said with fury, "and threaten the holiness of our plot.

What business have they there in our sanctified grove?

Their black bananas grow abundant in their own remote trove!"

"Precisely, Sir, precisely to the point",

The Jedic replied, rejoicing in his success at this joint.

"And as I'm bounding and jumping about,

This evil Moonie approaches me and starts to shout,

Raising on high the red bananas he took from my hands,

'A lovely gift indeed!', and without a qualm the bunch he commands.

As our beloved monarch promised, he claims it his own

And heaps words of praise upon King Brin and the throne!

Then he begins to speak words of such abomination,

Making statements drenched in detestation!"

"What words were they? Tell me now, instantly!

What abominations?" the Piglet demanded indignantly.

He looked anxiously at Rusty Jed, his response to hear,

Observing him hide from the sun in the branches near.

"Of a new forest he spoke, a forest illumined with light,

Which, as he claimed, King Brin had promised, much to their delight!

If my words be not the truth, my veracity impugned,

Let me be beheaded, my body by flames of fire consumed!

Behead me, burn me on a pyre!

The land is to be divided! To divide the land it will require!

He took the red bananas as a gift of commission,

A sign of the pledge's first partition!

The bananas he gave to the young ones, his laugh booming loud!

His eyes full of craving, his smile magnanimous and proud!

For our sacred grove he yearns, his eyes are focused there,

And the young ones chomp away happily without a care!

Our scarlet red bananas they greedily devour,

Their hunger never slackens, only growing by the hour!

To these horrific scenes my very eyes do testify,

Though the appetite of offspring one is bound to gratify!

And from where does the brightness of this forest come?

Will it bring upon us darkness, impervious and glum??

That is why I raced and hastened to return,

For evil thoughts must now become our foremost concern!"

"Silence at once! Say nothing more!" Pigletti angrily spoke,

Then sent a blow to the Jedic's face with a single forceful stroke.

 "Indeed you shall be beheaded, you can be certain of that!

Get on your way, don't show your face again, now scat!

Go to the blessed grove at once and pray with all your might

That I find truth in your words and your disloyal soul I won't smite!

For your many years of faithful service I will spare you now,

But don't assume that your protection they forever will endow!

With the moon-faced Black a visit I will arrange,

And won't bother the king with your words, satanic and strange!

Now leave at once and on your journey go!

My message will reach you when I decide it is so!"

Withdrawn, with head held low, the reddish one advanced through the thicketed wood,

And distanced himself from that illustrious tree just as fast as he could.

He felt happy and disappointed not one bit,

He'd deceived the Piglet with ease, he had to admit.

As horsemen they approached the kingdom's postern,
To announce a coup was their only concern.

A sprawling epistle they waved aloft,
One spoke sharply, the other spoke soft.

Its message to the king was very clear:
Let my people go, from far and near.

To set free and release this entire nation.
Refusal shall bring about complete desolation.

Holding a feather, glistening like dew,
He rushes to fulfill what he was sent to do.

Emitting beams of light, he forthwith conducts
The steps to be taken, and so instructs.

As he moves straight ahead on his singular course,
He is dominant, strict, with his haft strikes with force.

Unlike all others, he is of different mind,
Towards the innocent and weak he can be unkind.

His words are now contradicted well,
Orders are given to fight and rebel.

From the slopes of the Gilead he descends the hill,
With tongues of fire surrounding him still.

His brother approaches, with his hair so white,
To make peace he implores, and to set things right.

As evening falls his heart is kindled,
The frenzied look in his eyes hasn't dwindled.

Raging storms with mighty thunder assail,
Rocks are crushed, the people quail.

In din and uproar, on the winds he glides,
Holding the tablets, with clouds at his sides.

He lifts his hands skyward and then begins,
As this saga relates, to atone for sins.

9

"Slowly there, contemptable Red!
First bow deeply, then to the entrance tread!"

It was the voice of a monkey as black as night,
One of the Agagi's sentries, spotting the Red in his sight.

"It is the honorable Burakrati now approaching!"
His assistant informed the enemy, without encroaching.

"Then Burakrati, like all primates, his turn must wait
If he comes any closer, a blinding light will be his fate!"

The Burakrat and his aide felt their anger augmenting.
How could Norte's guards be so unconsenting?

This aide, with the Burakrat's help ever so subtle,
Allowed the Agagi every so often to enter and stir up trouble.

For weeks and months the Agagic Norte had paid the price,
Showering gifts and cash, to leave him to his device!

Now, having crossed over the border, fully exposed,

Shocked were they with such words to be opposed!

 "My dear friend, Burakrati, and his short-statured aide",
A weak yet authoritative voice now bade.

The senior sentinel escorts them along,
flinging them into a cave entry before long.

There, mounted on a horse, was the Agagi in all his splendor,
Displaying all the hatred and anger he could engender.

"Peace be with you, most valued partner and friend!"
The Burakrat quickly said, distressed at what this may portend..

The Agagic Norte, high upon his black horse, now halted,
Then with a slap to the Burakrat's face he assaulted.
"How dare you…" the aide stuttered then stopped,
As the senior one down to the ground had dropped.

The Agagi said not a word, but his sword he now drew
And grazed the Burakrat's head, drawing blood drops, just a few.

"It will be off with your heads, let there be no doubt!
If of your seditious actions I in due course find out!

Obscurati was quick the little ones to catch,
And even greater destruction went on to dispatch!
I am saying this now for the very last time,
My revenge will be tripled for your double-crossing crime!

The passages to the great waterhole must be open to us.
We are soon heading there, nothing more to discuss!"

Yet before he could remount his horse and be gone,
The Burakrat caught hold of his foot and held on.
"Our partnership is unique, my northern adversary!
Let us stay calm on this festive day, of our actions be wary!

In return for the precious stones, the passages I will open,
Your black monkeys' path guaranteed, your success unbroken!
The Moonies from the east will find it hard to enter,
From the Reds' Holy Grove the guards will never surrender.
And the Nabucottian has nothing but peace on his mind,
He has no interest in waging war, as you will find.
With an iron hand he rules the Moonies from the east,
It is impossible from his rule for them to ever be released!
The moon-faced monkeys are divided between the two,
But the Holy Grove they will never enter, it's so obviously true!
Now, let us once again swing from the highest trees,
We've yet to see the land of the great cedars, if you please!

And don't be so foolish as to challenge our primates blue,
One swoop of my hand and I split your black skull in two!
Remember this well, my dear collaborator, Nort,
With you I never sought to befriend or consort!

I will return now to the kingdom with my devoted aide.

Don't ever forget, our agreement is not to be betrayed!"

With that they quickly fled to a branch nearby,
And the Agagi's guards to pursue them didn't even try.
For without Burakrati, the Agagi's conspiring may yet fail,
So to harm him would be foolish and to no avail.

With his mind now made up, he mounted his horse,
Then headed northwest, keeping his course.

And the Gideonites upon the northern armies stormed,
From the depths a voice was heard, from black dust her words were formed.

From above, the golden rock is mightily crushed into slivers of light,
As the mountains of Gilead grow dim, cloaked in the darkness of night.

The armies attacked and their enemies scattered,
Their forces dashed and their spirits shattered.

And the divine voice will be heard once again,
Like a susurrant wind from the southern plain.

From on high the One shall appear and shield,
And from desolation and chaos again rebuild.

10

"Run, Brin, hurry, sprint over the branch! Your archrival comes near!

As fast as you can! We must attack and destroy, without dread or fear!"

His face damp, he shook himself awake from his dream,
As cold sweat dripped from his brow in a steady stream.

He now recalled how he himself had served in the Guard Corps!
What a strange dream, he hadn't dreamt anything like that before.

Indeed, he'd been the Corp's commander, of highest rank,
And hadn't seen a single peaceful day in this kingdom, to be frank.

And the enchanted grove, its magic lay in that its fruit
None other than the red monkeys were able to plant and root.

Numerous primate nations in this very place had once resided,
Yet none in picking a single red banana had ever prided.

The Grove serves the red monkeys alone and no other creature,
Its land continues fortifying them with one distinctive feature.

Now, as much as he may try, he cannot recall
A single quiet primate day in the kingdom, not at all.

The hour is ripe, it is time we change tracks,
Divide the Grove and share it with the Blacks!

And Nabucotti – he is always seeking peace,
His search for an opportune moment does not cease.

"Attack! Assail! The Holy Grove defend with all your might!
Run, Brin, Run! The enemy is darker than the blackest night!"

But now, awake from the nightmare that left him distrait,
He made his decision, determining Fate.

His ministers the following day he would reconvene,
To furtively plan strategic steps in the deep forest green.

To join forces together with the Nabucottian outright,
And the primate nations seek to unite.

On a nearby branch Obscurati now silently crouched,
The pipe in his mouth to his smugness avouched.

The discourse for sure he will keep surreptitious,
Yet will go on scheming without seeming suspicious.

As keeper of the gate, he will not remain still,

The Grove will never be divided, even if he must kill.

Under his influence, the advisor will be swayed,
His fury increased, the price will be paid.

The Grove is sacred, planted deep in his heart,
He is fully determined from it never to part.

He endowed their hearts, their minds united,
At which time the dictum will be expedited.

Turn not your attention away from him,
Hark closely to his words, their meaning do not dim.

He shall gather your souls around God's word,
Blessings and truth from his mouth shall be heard.

When struck by a plague grievous and hard,
Remain strong-hearted and be on your guard.

If you heed not these words, if they are scorned,
A torrential deluge shall ensue, be forewarned.

Do not turn your back on him, not for a moment brief,
He is not the enemy, but the bearer of sacred grief.

11

All bleary-eyed and sweaty,
Awoke the moon-faced Nabucotti.

He tucked in the sheets and made his bed,
Then washed his face and smoothed his head.

In the mirror, his reflection was sad to behold,
His eyes dark with worry of what the future may hold.

Something was paralyzing his mind with fear,
He had no clue as to what was drawing near.

Peeling a banana for his morning repast,
He heard the sound of many steps approaching fast.

He turned his head and went towards the door,
To see what was that noise that he couldn't ignore.

As he held on to the handle and gave one more glance,
A great crowd towards the citadel began to advance.

At the lead was none other than that infamous renegade,

Drawing a great crowd behind him, brazen, unafraid.

There was good reason for his sweaty sleepless night,
But it wasn't the unfolding of this sudden plight.

The Agagic Norte bowed down with head held low,
But in his eyes one could see a malicious glow.

He raised his hand and silenced the crowd,
Then turned to Nabucotti and said aloud:

"Greetings, our great and exalted leader",
But his voice sounded strange, a bit too eager.

"The forest is vast, its voice everyone hears,
The rumors fly and they hurt my ears."

"And what are these rumors that cause you anguish?
Are you seeking peace or are you looking to vanquish?"

"I come in peace, through and through.
But to the ones exploited what say you?
Their trees were downed, their honor dashed,
And you from the Reds take gifts, unabashed?"

The Moonie's heart is about to crumble,
But the gathering throngs won't make him tumble.

He must guard his royal honor and repute,

And won't give any ground to such dispute.

"How dare you address me with such impudent words!
Do you think you can scare me with this swarm of turds???
Shame on you, be gone, you ignominious fool!
A traitor you are! Do not challenge my rule!"

"And who does Your Majesty think you rule today?
These masses follow me, my word they will obey!
A treacherous king must pay with his life,
No petition allowed, there will be no more strife!
You have bowed before the ruddy ruler supreme,
You are a conniver, a foe, and so I deem!"

Nabucotti of the moon-faced monkeys thought to flee,
Yet sustained himself, despite the trembling in his knee.

With blasting sound the Blacks kept yelling loud,
Bent upon destruction with a quickly nearing crowd.

The moon-faced monkey then spoke up loud and clear,
To placate his people and thrust back the northern mutineer.

"You blackguard, you villain, you blithering fool!
Treaties are broken to defeat the enemy and rule!
Soft spoken and kind will my words increase and flow,
Then on the very branch we both were born, will come the
crushing blow!
Now about face and return to where you belong.

And I will look upon today as just a nightmare, a passing wrong!"

But Norte just stood and smirked with scorn.
To overturn the governance he was fully sworn.

The Moonie is outraged, he achieved his goal,
But before he retreats, he must bare his soul.

"Hear me well, my moon-faced monkeys in the east!
Your revered leader's honor is maintained, at the very least.
He speaks in our name, but it is in fact a ruse.
I am here for you, if your trust he will abuse.
To reach the Holy Grove now climb up and set about.
They've crushed our honor, to the not-so-distant we'll call out.
The Yellows our favor will help to restore,
For the Reds are their rivals, the Reds they abhor.
As to the Reds' fraternal mates who are very distant,
We will change their point of view if we remain persistent.

"Return to your perches on the branches and boughs,
Judgment Day is near, we have plans to espouse.
And once again begin the red bananas to destroy,
No peace will they have, nor their holidays enjoy.
Until throughout the jungle it becomes well known,
The red bananas, as inscribed, are the Blacks' alone!"

The growing gloom of darkness descended,
The malevolent followers it fully expended.

The wind whispered in their ear to intimidate,
Crush and destroy, for war is at the gate.

They seized one another to kill and assail,
Their swords held high to slash and impale.

The air was heavy with the smell of blood,
With the devil's sweat and gory mud.

Down the mountain the young boy raced,
Amongst torn garments and bodies defaced.

Westward he trod, true to his aim,
To his mother he headed, calling her name.

And the herald, her spirit to him will appear,
Westward and eastward, my young cavalier.

Through the desert sands he marched day and night,
Through cursed darkness and endless blight.

The wind as his guardian with him aligns,
He is destined to greatness, from birth he shines.

12

On a branch of the hyssop tree the Jedic reclines,
Thinking and plotting how he undermines.

How can he change the opinion of the horde?
Present the leader Nabucotti as a dangerous lord?

To him King Brin will pay no mind.
He wants only to divide. To all else he's blind.

He will then ask of the Piglet to be in accord,
And Burakrati will be told to faithfully record.

The Light Blues, Burakrati and Obscurati, are closely bound,
Their sworn allegiance to the Grove has always been profound.

Reddish Reds now gather in a wide circle to convene.
As Furrowed Brow and Curly Head loftily intervene.

Waiting for the tidings, for the final word replete,
Ready to take action, be it bitter, be it sweet.

"Listen well, my loyal Reds, with close devotion.

A most serious matter today is in motion!
Our sacred grove is so dear to your hearts, you all care.
Who is it that can say to you, 'No more!' Who would dare?!"

As he spoke, hushed whispers began,
He was talking of the Holy of Holies of the clan!

Some prominent elders try to interject,
But their efforts Curly and Furrow quickly reject.

"Indeed you heard well, make no mistake!
Dividing up the Grove, that's what is at stake!
And if you consider with our friends to divide",
Referring to the monkeys from the very-far side,
"If to share groves with the Blacks you are resolute,
They will sink their black teeth in our crimson red fruit!"

Now the tumult and noise cannot be contained,
By trying to stop them nothing will be gained.

On the contrary, let them work up their riotous tone,
At the moment, true solutions are better left alone.

Furrowed Brow and Curly with the notables will speak,
In gentle persuasion, and with no belligerence to seek.

Nearby, sits huddled in a cavernous tree
A dark brown primate, observing all he can see.

On this day, in his heart his plot starts to take shape,
To save those scarlet red bananas! There is no escape.

Just then Curly Head perceives him sitting there,
And climbs up to his side, him to prepare.

For the day of truth is drawing nigh,
As a foe the sovereign we will have to defy.

Terrifying, awesome days shall soon befall,
Most awesome and most terrifying of all.

Down the mountain, injuring his brothers on his descent,
His path is parched and dry and continues without end.

He picks up a stick, which path should be taken,
He seeks guidance and help, but is left forsaken.

And so he walks on towards the desert sands,
Heavy rains and Manna fill his outstretched hands.

His journey continues, he cannot turn back,
His path, like a smile, illuminates the black.

13

The great ruler Brin, thoughtful and tense,
Reviews in his mind the last days' events.

His advisors at once must be convened,
Explanations given, information gleaned.

Though intricate and complex is the issue at hand,
Division will supersede, it is his definitive stand.

Renowned forever will be these acts of transition,
He will change the forest beyond recognition.

For countless years to come, it will be spoken of and told
How Brin the King, in the square, brought tidings so bold.

He will gather the Reds and speak to them thus:
We'll have no more of wars, they have ended for us!

Our sacrifices will surely be taxing and great,
This must be explained, we must affirm and reiterate!

The Light Blues at the waterhole we needn't persuade,

They are willing and ready to share, unafraid.

But with the reddish Reds the challenge is hard,
They want the sacred grove to worship and guard.

Thus, with great caution plans should be contrived,
In consultation with others, our next steps derived.

Time is drawing near, foreseen the days ahead.
Division must be forced upon each and every Red.

And perhaps to the Agagi a message should be sent,
To dispatch to him forthwith our letter of intent.
To reach an accord and give him more groves,
And he too will be a friend, if it him behoves.

The letter Burakrati in person will convey,
His connections throughout the jungle will smooth his way.

He will soon be attending the meeting held next,
I should think of the speech and prepare the text.

And reveal to Burakrati our secret plans
Of sharing red groves with the Blacks, in advance.

But with Pigletti we must take special care,
He and the Jed are longtime chums. Beware.

From Rusty Jed our plans must stay concealed,

Till at the right moment they are to him revealed.

Brin, however, never thought, nor dreamed
That the Burakrat was not at all as what he seemed.

To Obscurati obedient and dutiful was he,
And both to the light blue monkeys were bonded secretly.

And Obscurati to the Piglet gave his loyalty with zeal.
 All news to him he would immediately reveal.

He would then summon the Jed in a quick maneuver
To have him ascertain and confirm the rumor.

His great satisfaction Burakrat can't suppress,
His plot's been launched with great success.

Clear instructions to the Curly he will dictate and put in place,
To arm that dark brown primate as the pursuer in the chase!

But for now it must all remain clandestine,
Continue to plot and bow to King Brin.

The days draw near like the toxic rain,
And the kingdom forever complete shall remain.

The Blacks come rushing down the slopes in hordes,
set out on a rampage to slay with their swords.

And the Lord God says unto them from on high,
Raise your hands up to the heavens, to the pure blue sky.

You will reach the mountain with no other but me,
To obey and hear my words that my son shall speak to thee.

Great stormy gusts of wind shall blow,
Drawing all your strength, never letting go.

What you seek and desire are profit and gold,
As reward for your heinous acts manifold.

As he nears the mount, a whisper will impart
A secret to his ear that will crush his heart.

Yet, again and again, the words he will distort,
Fearing, believing the edict he can thwart.

To him alone the words are said,
Pursued by the devil, forever in dread.

Just a wave of my hand and the devil shall flee,
On the day that your hearts are bound in unity.

14

 "And the cleaver must be blunt, is that clear?
That's what the dark-brown one will get, do you hear?!?"

The Piglet gives out orders and the instructions shouts,
Briefing Obscurati and explaining, to remove all doubts,

As to how and where Dark Brown with weapons is supplied.
In regard to all the rest, his fellow sentries will provide.

No chimp will discern what it is really all about.
A scapegoat will be found, cursed eternally as the lout!

All the planning clandestinely will be done,
Orders will be given with explanations none.

"Immediately after, we will place him inside the kangaroo,
And shout aloud, the finest of monkeys was downed by a coup!

Rush to the clinic, with no time to lose,
With Curly right behind, to further confuse."

"So it will be, honored Pigletti, Sir!

I will turn back to work, with the plans concur.
All will be ready, there's no time to lose,
Without explanations, with no excuse!"

He took leave of the Piglet his work to resume,
And disappeared swiftly in the forest gloom.

His mission he would complete well concealed,
Knowing that the Burakrat would serve as his shield.

Having waited for months for this one command,
The hour of sedition was now at hand.

And that other will then turn to the cunning Rusty Jed,
Shouting out loud, "Furrowed Brow and Curly Head!"

And all be recorded in whispers, to make sure
That this most complex and momentous act is secure.

The Jedic, though taken by surprise, will have no say,
He'll have to choose between life and death on that day!

His authority will fail him on this Judgment Day.
His rank and command will have no sway.

Obscurati and the Burakrat on a wave of power surge,
Using lies and falsehoods, and as heroes will emerge.

The groves shall never be divided, not ever,

It will be seen to, behind the scenes, through every endeavor.

Now pay mind to the words of the wise,
Bow deeply, listen and internalize.

And little monkeys climbed and grew,
And turned into humans, without much ado.

The more prominent to the cave of knowledge arrive,
To share whispered secrets they eagerly strive.

Squatting in a corner, one mortal waits to hear
A little bird, a harbinger, that will whisper in his ear.

His wisdom is as rich as resplendent gold,
The tidings, the gospel, to him alone are told.

He leaves the cave and the place where he stands,
And heads to a retreat through the desert sands.

His heart finds shelter in the desert's expanse,
It is he who knows the plot's unfolding in advance.

As plotted, the turbaned king shall be taken
To the golden gates of Heaven, and there forsaken.

The little one crouches, his task he doesn't shun,

He stabs and jabs at the heart of the most admired one.

Thus a scepter in his hand he holds,
To sever and shatter what his heart beholds..

15

"Greetings to you, Agagi, most revered!"
Said the governor, whose color was somewhat weird.

A strange canary yellow, of a somewhat shiny strain,
As was common in the not-so-distant cold domain.

"I here grant you this gift, Governor and friend",
And a bunch of black bananas the Agag placed in his hand.

Here we must emphasize once more and underscore,
These bananas were of the finest that ever were before.

The Blacks by the canary Yellows were always adored,
Supported and helped, for the Reds they abhorred.

At every happenstance that would come their way,
The Reds they would vilify and slander without delay.

Share the grove with the Blacks, that's the conception,
The Agagi is right and free of deception.

For the Yellows, the chronicles stated it clear and sublime,

The grove was sacred to them since the dawn of time.

"My canary yellow friend, to you I have come.

The situation is harsh and succor I have none.

The inhabitants of the jungle with the Reds unite,

The great very-far region's voice pounds in my head day and night.

I bring news from just a week ago, from northern border locations,

Where the Reds ravaged black banana groves with repeated violations.

The little ones they knocked about, the precious trees they downed,

The black bananas of our livelihood crushed cruelly to the ground.

It is with a great sense of shame that I appeal to you, my friend,

A supplication for your help to see this matter penned."

The Canary Yellow well perceives the circumstance,

It is time to create a legend, it is a great chance.

This epic tale he will recount without further delay,

Showing sympathy to the Blacks, so his words will convey.

And when the day comes and the time is ripe,

He will be rewarded with oil-black bananas of the finest type.

Such a plethora of black bananas in the jungle have the Blacks,

They will gladly share with him if he the Reds' repute attacks.

"Agagi, my dear friend, I fully concur, it is a fine solution.

A report of the hateful Reds will be written as a resolution.

Throughout the forest it shall be duly heard and fittingly explained

How you were exploited, subjugated, yet so brave and self-restrained!

It is time to push the Reds back where they belong,

To return to the Blacks what is theirs, with spirits strong!

And of the very-far-region's monkeys I have no need,

How hateful and contemptible they are indeed!

But to their habitat gallop through the forest quickly,

And pour out your lament before them briskly.

The very-far-region monkeys have impact on the Reds.

Cursed be the bond that between them weds!

With Brin they will build a dream to coexist,

And from dividing the grove they will not desist.

As for the Holy Grove, just leave it in my hands,

My comrades and I will implement plans.

Without delay the news you will hear,

The red groves will be divided, have no fear.

I accept your offer and welcome your gesture,

Brin's kingdom will soon be yours, it's no longer a conjecture!"

On that night a voice calls out loud and clear,

Your cry to the heavens he doesn't hear.

That night in great numbers you shall be slayed,
The eternal memory of this ignominy shall never fade.

With swords in their hands they wield their power,
And snatch up young maidens, as if picking a flower.

There they march in lines long and straight,
Being led to the slaughter, to their untimely fate.

On this darkest of days, at the hour allocated,
The final solution, his seed eradicated.

Pitch black are the skies, gone is the sun,
Ashes spiral upward, smoke pillars of dun.

Like cattle, like mules, you are silently led,
No redeemer at hand, it is off with your head.

To the Promised Land go forth, the hour is nigh,
Like grains of sand you shall flourish and multiply.

You shall come together, like a column of swirling sand,
An olive branch shall drift from on high, down to the land.

Like a mother's nectar, like flowing milk and honey,
An eternal covenant with this land I shall give to thee.

16

To the center of the light blue waterhole they come,
A chorus briskly marching to the beat of the drum.

Dressed in orange, purple, pink and green,
On the marching-ground they now convene.

The voice of many choirs is heard all about,
The forest path is cleared, there's no going in or out.

Hansoms filled with joyous monkeys on their way,
Moving to and from the waterhole with commuters to convey.

At that precise moment, with no forewarning,
A fearsome noise pierced the air of the morning.

Frightening and loud as that noise might be,
The scene that unfolded was more chilling to see.

Parts and bits of monkeys were strewn upon the trees,
The stench of scorched flesh was carried in the breeze.

A great commotion started, and was moving out of control

At the very center of this grand light blue waterhole.

"Who could have set off the fuze so well?"
Voices in the forest began to swell.

And every life-loving monkey quickly made haste
To his own abode and habitat, with no time to waste.

Here reside light blue monkeys of prestigious kin,
Blood relations of the good King Brin.

A tumultuous noise spread through the forest by increasing degree,
Who can this audacious enemy be?

Bent on causing us harm, destructive and wild,
Making no distinction between fighter and child.

In the center of the parade he had decided on the spot,
And chose this light blue waterhole from the entire lot.

From the depth of the forest new voices were now heard,
"Off with their heads, Norte, Nabucotti and the Moonie herd!"

The kingdom was in turmoil, both on left and right,
Swept with fury and anger, with no end in sight.

The Piglet and the Burakrat are quick to climb the tree,
To meet with Brin who was pacing frantically.

"Pigletti, Sir, I will hear your report without further delay,
We've suffered defeat in the heart of our kingdom today!"

"A heavy price they will surely pay for this attack!
I will crush the Moonies so, they won't ever come back!"

"Be silent, Commander, if you please!
Answer me directly without hyperboles.
I want your report and immediate reply,
There is one responsible for this, to whom does that apply?"

"Most honored Brin, my beloved king.
Developments from east and north I bring.
The blue waterhole they wish to destroy,
And blacken the Holy Grove, using every ploy.
To negotiate they pretend to be inclined,
But then will stab your blue back from behind.
Your soul seeks brotherhood, in peace to dwell.
Brave acts and warring you've known too well.
You wish to end bloodshed and see it no more,
But in your heart you know we're on the brink of war.

And if you try to delay, postponement to engender,
It will be perceived as weakness and clear surrender.
We must rise and uproot them at this very hour,
And show the hooligan Blacks who's in power!"

"Pigletti my friend, calm yourself, pay heed.

You seem possessed right now, there is no need.

What is in your heart I understood,

I followed your wishes as best I could.

Yet the days are now drawing near

With winds of war blowing clear.

I will choose a different path to take,

And no longer send troops my enemy to break.

For we and they are all primates the same,

And all wish our livelihood to reclaim."

"What they wish for is your heart, beloved King!

And your kingdom to crush, leaving not one thing.

From the very first day of this kingdom we adore

They've been gathering power and mongering war.

And those sudden attacks, you certainly recall,

On our day of fast, our holiest day of all.

Their tongues speak nothing but deception and lies,

Their placating words are but a disguise.

To the Canary Yellows they will surely turn,

With the oil-black bananas their trust will earn.

Throughout the jungle they have many brothers,

Our tiny kingdom is nothing, compared to others.

They are trying to bring us down to ruination,

And take our Holy Grove without approbation.

They've but themselves to blame, by their choices bound.

It is kill or be killed, we must stand our ground.

At the blue waterhole the blue monkeys bide,

They don't understand, but agree to divide.
Not until they were attacked and harmed,
Did they think to protect their borders, alarmed.
They're willing to divide the land without a thought,
Our heritage for them has come to naught.
And now, our wise King Brin, the most noble of names,
Have you too forgotten what the charter proclaims??"

In his royal perch, King Brin remained withdrawn.
His senior minister angry at his lack of brawn.

He understood him well and all that he held fast,
And his love for his kingdom nothing else surpassed.

Yet in his heart the die had been cast a long time ago.
Division was a must, at the square he'll declare it so.

 "Pigletti, my dear friend, let me tell you what I think.
Confrontations and war will only lead us to the brink.
Our good land, though small, must be divided,
Thus more Black aggression will never be ignited.

With the very-far region I have often spoken,
They will give guarantees that won't be broken.
The choice is no longer for us to decide,
Throughout the jungle all will abide."

He then quickly swung from tree to tree,
The Moonies' ruler immediately to see,

Leaving the Piglet in his fury to stew,
Upset and angry, with no further ado.

And before the people two emissaries stood,
Ezekiel the Mad and Gracie the Good.

Espousing advice and suggestions galore,
Of the people to follow and heed they implore.

Ezekiel the Mad shouts out in anger,
"Forsake your oaths", he says with rancor,

"Like sheep led to pasture on that fateful day,
Through the desert sands you went astray.

How can your Lord have forsaken his nation,
And condemn you to years of hard work and oppression."

Then Gracie the Good rose up to speak,
Giving forth hope, saying nothing bleak.

"Your God is forgiving and your sins atoned,
Though you've abandoned your Lord and Him disowned.

You shall be forgiven, your people redeemed,
Your seed multiplied beyond anything you dreamed.

You shall be numerous as the grains of sand,
And embrace the Lord in the Promised Land.

Wells shall fill with sweet water your thirst to quench,
And swell to a river, the land to drench.

Afflicted by other nations, you shall not surrender,
You shall dwell on the land in peace and splendor.

And united you shall be and declare as one,
"It is the word of God and His will be done."

17

"Welcome, dear friend", the king of Blacks said to Brin.
"What a pity on happier occasions we don't convene."

"The situation is grave, it must be stayed.
How distressing that our mission will be delayed."
"Indeed what was done was most severe.
But I cannot keep order as yesteryear.
Reds from the north chose the little ones to attack,
And the word was out to revenge and pay back."

"That exactly is what I wish to discuss.
How was this kept a secret from us?"

"Brin, my brother, my dearest friend.
To decapitate me is what they intend!
The friendship we share outrages them so,
And what the populace feels you, more than all others, know."

"Unfortunate it is, a touchy issue at that,
Which we must with courage arise to combat.
Primates of many colors live in my domain,

This is the hour that our fearlessness shall reign.
The Moonies look up to you to lead,
You must meet the challenge, you cannot cede.
Can you serve as a leader, as a Head of State,
If one ruffian alone can your rule truncate?
From that imbecile what is it that sets you apart?
He despises the Reds, seeks no peace in his heart.
The moment has come, put your life on the line,
Your greatness and stature to Fate now consign."

"Oh, my dear Brin, my wonderful friend.
If only your greatness I could transcend.
Though my head is willing, my heart is askew.
I am nothing but a cleric, no pioneer like you.
The little ones I can educate and in them invest,
But the adults' hatred weighs heavy on my chest.
Our mission lies fully on your shoulders alone,
May you be blessed and save our kingdom and throne."

Incensed and outraged was he as never before,
The Promised Land must remain undivided evermore.

Fearless and with conviction he quickly dispatched
Wild hawks, fierce falcons and vampire bats.

He felt one with the Lord and that was the key,

At peace with himself, no traitor was he.

But his sharp mind, diminished with time,
Led him to commit an unfathomable crime.

18

This is the plan, well-devised and precise.
As he mingles with the crowd, a loud cry will suffice.

His great cry of grievance will be heard by all,
Entering their hearts, never to pall.

The danger is great, at our doorstep it lies.
Never a division, and no compromise!

Only by fear will he get his message through,
No friend is he, and with a façade untrue.

From the beginning of time it was an untenable dream,
To even eye the red bananas was an unfeasible scheme.

With deceit we will scare them and get our way,
The Burakrat plotted, fully ready for the fray.

After the Piglet completes his needed rest,
He will approach him and talk at his behest.

Every step must be so very wisely taken,

Nor can the Minister of Police be forsaken.

The Dark Brown one is to be squarely blamed,
As monstrous and hostile, completely untamed.

The Reds, the Dark-Browns too, we'll cast suspicion on the lot,
So as to guard against exposing the secret plot.

The doctors' silence will be bought, to their gain.
Of the source of the wounds no proof will remain,

No clue shall be left of their location or size,
For nothing took place, they can only surmise.

The nation as one shall grieve and deeply mourn,
And he who asks, as a mad rebel will be accused with scorn.

With Obscurati no one dares to deal,
And with Pigletti – for sure it's an ordeal!

The Piglet will advise Obscurati of his part in the stunt,
To equip the Dark-Brown one with a knife that is blunt.

No one will take notice of what will then ensue,
For the Blues will seat a healthy Brin into the kangaroo.

To the nearest clinic they will arrive after some delay,
"Watch out! Watch out!" Curly will shout aloud and make way.

No one will perceive what really did take place,

That after the 'stabbing', Brin did an about-face

To see what the commotion was all about and why,
Then was literally stabbed in the back, without further hue or cry.

None know what the kangaroo pouch enfolds,
Concealment a great commotion upholds.
Rusty Jed witnesses the scene that unfolds
And screams from the horror that he beholds.

The Piglet takes the lead and shouts out his commands.
"Stab from the back, like Dark Brown did!" he now demands.

"But there is a stab wound in the chest, don't you see?"
"No one will check", the blue one placates, "not in a decade, nor in three!"

Brin, still alive, calls out for help with great urgency,
"Have you betrayed me too, my dear friend Burakrati?!"

Then to Pigletti he turns, trying to understand,
"You were my brother, and to my murder you gave a hand?"

But he was faced with only blank expressions that nothing testified,
"With the Nabucottian you had planned the groves to divide!"

"The Middle Kingdom, the Sacred Red you have betrayed!
You conspired towards division with the wicked Moonie's aid!"

With his dying breath, Brin spoke his last words, unafraid:
"Peace must be achieved, and with one's enemies is made."

But King Brin no longer was in Pigletti's view,
Who was busy sermonizing and yelling at the Blue.

This task must be ended, whatever it may require,
But his eyes, oh, his eyes, they were burning like fire!

And Rusty Jed, who hadn't been included in the know,
Felt compelled to shout as well and followed now in tow.

"Stab from the back!" he yells, as if trying to redress,
"No one will check!" Obscurati says, "Who dares with Burakrati to mess???"

Pigletti will threaten those whose obedience may slouch,
and Kangaroo, though unharmed, has a deep red stain in his pouch.
Blame will be placed on the Dark Brown, and on him alone,
He's a crazy one, out to impress, wishing to be known.

And he rose up, and struck him, and struck him still.
He rose up again, all the goodness to kill.

On the slope down to Hades his tears didn't cease,

Like an innocent babe grieving over his caprice.

The wisest of men cannot fathom nor comprehend
How to such villainous abomination one could descend.

19

In the Middle Kingdom on this very day,
A male and female primate together made their way.

To the young one with them they give a helping hand,
To light a candle and observe from where they stand.

And the young one gathers others round the candlelight,
For their grief is profound, their hearts seek to unite.

There at the site they sat on wooden benches,
All about them blockades so that no one entrenches.

"My fellow primates, I have come here to say,
There has never been a more tragic and mournful day.
A traitor to our kingdom to the gallows will be led,
None shall come near him, his evil is widespread.
This is the hour our strength to unite,
Our courage to embrace and put our differences aside.
This infamous day will be remembered for all time,
Now let us bow our heads, and up the mountain climb!"

Burakrati this message to the trembling masses brought,
All were holding candles and sharing one thought.

Take revenge on the devil, it must be carried out.
There is no stepping back and no room for doubt.

Whosoever dares Burakrati to thwart,
With a single glance will be staved off and cut short.

And one Rusty Jed moves restlessly about, shaken, deeply sored,
With mind-numbing grief over the king he so adored.

True, to dethrone him he sought, and he did so conspire,
But an act such as this, that was never his desire!

Alongside him Curly and the Brow walk with steps constrained,
Their thoughts tormented and their energies drained.

The Burakrat and the Piglet played their hand in determining fate,
Exploiting their power, their own will to sate.
The threesome now sat in a circular huddle,
Up high in the tree, afar from the muddle.

"Listen closely, my good friends, to what I say,
Interrupt me not, till my thoughts I convey!

Your trust in me is vital, I need you to be true.
We've been deceived and lied to, I didn't have a clue!

Now we must carefully consider and deliberate
If to act against the Burakrat, the three of us collaborate."

"But," Curly Head inquired, "how can it be done?
"The Piglet and Burakrati have control of everyone.
Whoever says a word with a shadow of misgiving
Will find himself quite quickly no more among the living."

"Dear friends, look here, all our reddish Reds we will unite,
Then secretly encourage them to accept what's right.
Nothing will be said and naught will be revealed
Of our goal to save the Dark Brown one, our lips are sealed.
For one who sits in a dungeon for a crime he didn't do,
Darkens our souls, with the mark of Cain upon us too.
Return now quickly as you naturally were,
We will help Burakrati rule, and with his wish concur.
But understand this well, the hour will surely come,
We will obey and follow to the beat of the drum!"

The high cliffs shall break and tumble,
And the trees at their roots shall crumble.

Lightning shall pierce the heavenly vault,
And thunderbolts the deep oceans assault.

The waters shall rise forty cubits higher,
And the queen to her kingdom shall forthwith retire.

The people their eyes to the heavens ascend,
The tidings like a bolt of lightning descend.

Half of the desert in deep silence remains,
His solitary voice carried across the plains.

She will appear to the dreamers in all her splendor,
As madmen their visions of her will them render.

They shall come to the wizard his advice to follow,
But their many words the mountain shall swallow.

Exulted and great is their image in her reflection,
The completeness of the nation is transcended by her perfection.

They stride on the waves, which carry with first light
A soft divine voice and a bird in flight.

Like a splendid princess, hers is a gift of wonder,
Her tidings forever prevail, with a legacy like no other.

A sandstorm rages as she approaches out of yore,
In exile seven hundred years and decades four.

And messianic forces around her shall abound,
the Land of Judah, the promised ground.

EPILOGUE

"Back to your loathsome task this instant",
The winged one with the bristled hair was persistent.

"Sharpen the beak, and the chisel turn.
Once again!" he commanded, arrogant and stern.
Northwest of this post, a sharp-beaked crow,
Infrastructure Minister, observed all below.

With every word this thin-winged bird would utter,
The forest in its entirety would shudder.

Once again, with a probing eye he checks, is unsure.
That brash one, should he suspect him or feel secure?

His kingdom is filled with unwelcome bats
Who loot and plunder the crows' habitats.

"Return immediately! Tomorrow at dawn",
He said disparagingly, with an offensive yawn.

To the east he turned a sharp focused look,
Observing Speckle for as long as it took.

Through a cunning ploy with a surprising boom,
He will conquer the forest in silence and gloom.

In his wake the forest will turn barren and bare,
Shrouded in desolation, stillness everywhere.

Carrions and carcasses will be spread far and wide,
At the center of that grove so loved and glorified!

"Thaw him out. Thaw out that strange bird!"
Speckle, the black raven, ordered, undeterred.

The yellow-beaked Speckle was king of kings,
Of the finest species of all flocks on wings.

"Take him down a bit", his aide, the grand pelican, instructed
And his workers themselves accordingly conducted.

"Is that not His Majesty, the revered King Brin…
From the frost and ice come forth now, return.
Two thousand years you have rested in peace.
But it is time to awaken, your death to surcease!"

"Two thousand years? Who determined so and why?"
King Brin wondered silently as he opened one eye.

"Two thousand years, to be precise and exact,
The high-ranking echelons have so recorded as a fact."

"And peace, yes, there is peace, I believe?"
Brin asked in a tone ingenuous and naïve.

"Peace? Ah, piecemeal is what I think you mean!"
He mockingly replied, with a play on words a bit obscene.

"And the Reds? And the Blacks? Where are they now?"
Brin asked, expecting to learn somehow.

"They killed one another, all are lost,
Peace has departed, out the window tossed.
Piece by piece", he chuckled naughtily.
"Yes, all went to pieces", he now laughed with glee.

"Then why awaken me, if what you say is so,
Why show me my world, lost so long ago?"

"Ah, Brin, my dear good-hearted friend,
You must stand with me, your wisdom to lend.
Throughout my reign I've seen you only asleep.
I have waited for just the right time to reap.
Now is the hour, as droves of bats us attack,
Day and night these clawed devils keep coming back.
And we ravens, who are of short crest and wing,
An end to this awful avalanche must bring.

And you, the wisest of all primates, my friend
I've awakened to repulse them and bring to their end."

"Well I understand, my short-crested friend,
But my own nation I could not save, to the bitter end.
Had I been successful in fulfilling my role,
We would have no need of this conversation at all."

The speckled raven then lowered his crest,
And pulled his short wings in, close to his chest.

In his heart he knew that this king, so kind,
Wished to protect him, to love was inclined.

"Your mission will succeed, the distrustful put aside,
My forces are faithful and stand strong at my side!"

"My friend, I have but one piece of advice to share.
Watch out for the fools, and from advisors beware!"

Like countless grains of sand the days are begotten,
No voice shall respond, all names are forgotten.

As the wise they come, foremost a deed to do,
They harken with care, and wish to carry through.

Vessels and scrolls from ancient ground are exhumed,
From foreign lands a mass return is resumed.

As they anoint themselves with oils and light,
Their vulgar acts are hidden from their own sight.

The finest emissaries, of exulted rhetoric and speech,
Shunned and forgotten, they seek to impeach.

And darkness, like a membrane, covers their eyes.
To devastate, destroy, to break and ostracize.

Their hearts do not long for deeds to be done,
As in those commandments from days long gone.

From the heavens above the Jesuit prophet was sent,
His body bruised, his heart cruelly rent.

Till the end of time they shall wait evermore,
Abominations, denunciations and mongering war.

The strong shall win, humiliating the weak,
To Hades they are led, broken and meek.

At the dawn of a new and blessed time,
That very same kingdom prevails, sublime.

ABOUT THE AUTHOR

Aviv Geva

"Imagine you're in a really good relationship, everything's really good and nice and you love each other, but they promise you that with someone else it would be the love of your life. If they swore to you that this was the case, how many of you would get up and leave?

In Dr. Seuss's book 'Cat in the Hat', the children are left alone at home. Being bored, they want to do something fun. But they mustn't, it is forbidden... Then who appears out of nowhere? The cat in the hat! He fulfils everything they asked for despite the fact that the fish in the jar warns the children that their mother will be very angry!

Throughout our entire lives we want and ask from the universe or from God all sorts of things. To fulfil dreams, to realize fantasies. But most of the time we are too afraid or rely on the fears of others. "But how?", "But it's impossible", "But how many succeed??"

I was a lawyer. I Hated myself. Hated my life. I started writing totally 'by chance', as they say. A former screenwriter that studied with me in my first law degree thought that I was talented and that I should give it a try.

I wrote about thirty pages and forgot all about it. Two years later, again 'by chance' of course, I met this girl I knew years before and that was now some kind of psychic. After two minutes of small-talk she suddenly asked out of the blue - "maybe you wrote something?".

At first I said no, because I didn't even remember it, but then I told her that in fact I did. "That's your purpose in life," she immediately replied, "you'll be a great Author."

That conversation totally 'flipped me over' because there wasn't the slightest chance she could have known about it.

As time went by I completed my first novel, but no publisher wanted it. An unknown writer, not a celebrity or something like that, why should they take a chance?

But I wasn't going to give up. And despite the fact that I was already quite respectful divorce-mediation lawyer and even taught divorce-mediation in Bar-Ilan university, I took a chair and a folding table, and sat in the middle of the main street of Tel-Aviv selling my book to passers-by, when all my surrounding thought I got fucked up in the head...

But that wasn't the hardest part. Even though I started getting very good reviews and letters from readers in social media, I couldn't have my books be sold at bookstores because the distributors didn't want to take a chance with a self-published book.

It took as much as three years, but eventually people started asking for my book at the bookstores. Within two more years my first novel became a best-seller, and just recently I have published my fifth book.

So don't ever let anyone tell you something is not possible, and I really hope you'll enjoy my writings.

With lots of love,

Aviv."

*

Social media:

Instagram: @avivgeva

Facebook: Author Aviv Geva

Twitter: @avivgeva

BOOKS BY THIS AUTHOR

The Knight Is A Son Of A Bitch

AN ISRAELI BESTSELLER

"Have you ever asked yourselves if you believe in love at first sight? I never asked and was never eager to find out. I was living in a world where my biggest challenges surrounded work, whether or not to call a specific girl, loving my boss, hating her, or ignoring her. Dying to fuck her on the conference room table or up against the photocopier in the corridor, not capable of touching her with a guide dog for the blind -- regular and mundane matters of any normal person in his twenties. It never occurred to me that I would concern myself with fateful questions, questions of life and death. I certainly didn't imagine that this would be my life or death. I most definitely didn't imagine that I would choose death. But if I hadn't been preoccupied with choosing the preferable way of dying, it seems I would never have known if there is such a thing as love at first sight or not. Were it not for the intervention of the God of Fates himself, I would have been just another guy who had never felt anything in his life, who never experienced the most enchanted moment of all. Suddenly, every refusal of hers is interpreted as a nod. Every receding step seems like lips drawing closer for a kiss. There blows the Goddess of Love and Emotion and a fix of her hair makes your heart skip a beat. A fraction of a smile is everything you could ever wish for. And so, when you but allow this wandering spirit in front of you to acknowledge that this very moment the moon is shining down on the most beautiful evening of her life, you suddenly understand that all the rejections in your life so far have been nothing but pleading smiles, that knew deep down in their hearts that your love wasn't meant for them, but for her alone.

One thing is certain, no matter how much you will be told otherwise. Behind every common womaniser stands a woman who has ripped his heart apart."

Reviews:

"Psychotic borderline brilliance" —Sara Rachmiel Book Reviews

"Aviv gives us a real understanding of how a man's brain works" —Blogger Odelia Tzadok

"Mistakenly, I thought that this was a book that easily entered the genre of 'flight books', but when I read – or rather, got sucked into it – I realized that it was not the case – but the exact opposite. 'The Knight is a Son of a Bitch' contains philosophical and existential elements that ask the reader questions about his condition, surroundings, emotions and feelings. It is a book that raised questions within me about solipsism and touched me at extraordinary depths. I do not know if Geva, the author of this important work, is aware of his unique talent, as an author, or in this case to be precise, as a "story teller" – and to the many tiers that his writing contains." —Author Doron Braunshtein

"The authors ability to cast his hero in different dimensions of time, in extreme degrees of recognition and understanding, within a spectrum of emotions that has more colors than the rainbow flag, attests to one thing: Something unusual takes place between these pages" — Bookmark Books Recommendations

"From the first moment, the blunt language is a wonderful mask and a literary tool that serves the plot perfectly. I would not be ashamed to say genius" —Author Osnat Saban

"A different point of view and writing, so real and so true, so many passages in the book I couldn't say good-bye to! Writing that has everything, the book made me laugh, cry, get angry and think endlessly about life... The book won't leave my heart any time soon"—Author Eleanor Lugasi

"Honest, touching, melancholic but strangely uplifting, it was a fantastic read."—Author Edward Evans

Draggy The Dragon

World's largest creative network 'Behance' main medal award for illustrations!
"One day, Draggy decided, out of the blue,
That to scare innocent people he no longer wished to do.

He would put out his fire and keep his mouth shut,
And no longer remain in the scary dragon's rut.

But what will he do now? How will he loom large?
All eyes are on Terrible Draggy, waiting for him to charge.

And all he really wants is to find a lovely dragon lass
And build with her a little home on a little patch of grass."

*

"A children's book with mature intentions. I love the little dragon who experienced a change, a change that is not easy, to stop burning and be kind = different and special. With a loving friend who supports him in the essential change. I recommend the book to all the little "dragons" who discover a difficult change, but it is also possible and rewarding. For them and their parents who support them in the blessed change."

Review by Ahuva Oberstein at "Nurita" book reviews website

☆☆☆☆☆

"You will have to read this lovely book! The book enables a conversation with children about social pressure, about the possibility of change and that change, even if it is difficult, is blessed. The story and the lovely drawings that match the text captured the hearts of my grandchildren who did not leave the book all weekend! At the end of the book there are two coloring pages that definitely add interest.

I Highly recommend!"

Review by Panina Aharonov at "Nurita" book reviews website

☆☆☆☆☆

"A wonderful book for children that provides insights and morals that adults can also adopt. The fear of not being accepted, the lifestyle of doing what is expected even if it goes against the inner self, the desire to please and be loved because of conventions established by society. Bottom line: First of all, love and believe in yourself. Do only what is good for you and not what you think will make others love you. Those who love you will continue to love you even with all your shortcomings. Highly recommended!"

Book recommendations Sarah Rahmiel

☆☆☆☆☆

"'Draggy the Dragon' is essentially a children's book, however, in my opinion, it is in fact - in its insights and the wide-ranging intellectual morality it contains - a novel for adults: thick-skinned, incredibly smart, and above all - multiple meanings, duality and symbolism. This is one of those books that while reading them, and upon the end of reading them, the reader will better understand their genius and depth, and at the same time, the many-faceted textual ambition that are hidden in them."

Marvelee

"What shall I do, my Marvelee, once you have grown?
Perhaps the march of time we can freeze or postpone?"

REVIEWS:

"… The book is so enchanting, wise and entertaining, that it easily deserves the title of "The sweetest children's book published in 2018"
Chai-tarbut Book Reviews
☆☆☆☆☆

"Aviv Geva has succeeded, with great charm and sensitivity, in telling a story about the ties between a father and his little girl in a wonderfully delightful and moving way!
The perfect gift for every dad. I highly recommend it!!"
Book Reviews – Sara Rachmiel
☆☆☆☆☆

"This is a children's book that is a kind of confession of a new father about his feelings for his first child and his sense of wonder at the arrival of an "marvelous" girl who changed his life and feelings. A love story that every new parent will be able to identify with. Written in language suitable for children, the charming illustrations blend beautifully with the text, I think Children will love to hear the book especially when dad reads it to them and changes the name of "Marvelee" to the name of his boy or girl."

Review by Sima Ofir on "Nurita" book revies website
☆☆☆☆☆

"Wow, what an exciting book and stunning in its beauty, a book that is entirely dedicated to the new father or to the future father to his daughter... It is structured in short paragraphs, punctuated and rhymed, the colorful and spectacularly beautiful illustrations cause you to be drawn in, fall in love and be moved by the entire charming story... I wholeheartedly recommend About this wonderful book, a book that I enjoyed so much reading to my little granddaughters, who did not want to part with it and asked to continue reading it more and more... At the end of the book, our little children are given the opportunity to color in the two attached coloring pages, an experience in itself that will add value to reading and looking through the entire book .. just lovely!"

Review by Yehudit Began on "Nurita" book revies website

Printed in Dunstable, United Kingdom

64389354R00071